Band of Cahuilla • Ak-Chin Indian Community • Akiachak Native Community • Akiak Native Commu[...] Tribe of
Algaaciq Native Village • Allakaket Village • Alturas Rancheria • Alutiiq Tribe of Old Harbor • Ango[...] Anvik
Atqasuk Village • Augustine Band of Cahuilla Indians • Bad River Band of Lake Superior Tribe of Chippewa Indians • Barona Band
Village • Berry Creek Rancheria Tyme Maidu Tribe • Big Lagoon Rancheria • Big Pine Paiute Tribe of the Owens Valley • Big Sandy
Creek Tribe • Bishop Paiute Tribe • Blackfeet Nation • Blue Lake Rancheria • Bridgeport Indian Colony • Brothertown Indian Nation • Buena
• Caddo Nation • Cahto Tribe • Cahuilla Band of Indians • California Valley Miwok Tribe • Campo Kumeyaay Nation • Catawba Indian Nation •
Wampanoag Tribe • Cheesh-Na Tribe • Chemehuevi Indian Tribe • Cher-Ae Heights Indian Community of the Trinidad Rancheria • Cher-O-
of Georgia Tribal Council • Chevak Native Village • Cheyenne and Arapaho Tribes • Cheyenne River Sioux Tribe • Chickahominy Indian Tribe •
California • Chignik Bay Tribal Council • Chignik Lake Village • Chilkat Indian Village (Klukwan) • Chilkoot Indian Association (Haines) • Chinik
of Louisiana • Choctaw Nation • Choctaw-Apache Tribe of Ebarb • Chuloonawick Native Village • Circle Native Community • Citizen
Coeur D'Alene Tribe • Coharie Tribe • Cold Springs Rancheria of Mono Indians of California • Colorado River Indian Tribes • Colusa
Tribes of the Flathead Reservation • Confederated Tribes and Bands of the Yakama Nation • Confederated Tribes of Coos, Lower
the Chehalis Reservation • Confederated Tribes of the Colville Reservation • Confederated Tribes of the Umatilla Indian Reservation
Indians • Cowlitz Indian Tribe • Coyote Valley Band of Pomo Indians • Craig Tribal Association • Crow Creek Sioux Tribe • Crow Tribe
Band of Pomo Indians • Duckwater Shoshone Tribe • Duwamish Tribe • Eastern Band of Cherokee Indians • Eastern Pequot Tribal Nation •
• Edisto Natchez-Kusso Tribe of South Carolina • Egegik Village • Eklutna Native Village • Elem Indian Colony of Pomo Indians • Elk Valley
(Yuchi) Tribe • Evansville Village (Bettles Field) • Ewiiaapaayp Band of Kumeyaay Indians • Fallon Paiute-Shoshone Tribe • Federated Indians
Community • Fort Independence Indian Community of Paiute Indians • Fort McDermitt Paiute and Shoshone Tribes • Fort McDowell Yavapai
Winds Tribe, Louisiana Cherokee • Galena Village (Louden Village) • Georgia Tribe of Eastern Cherokee • Gila River Indian Community • Golden
Band of Ottawa and Chippewa Indians • Greenville Rancheria • Grindstone Indian Rancheria of Wintun-Wailaki Indians • Guidiville Rancheria
Tribe • Hannaville Indian Community • Havasupai Tribe • Healy Lake Village • Herring Pond Wampanoag Tribe • Ho-Chunk Nation • Hoh Tribe
Indians • Hualapai Tribe • Hughes Village—Hodotl'eekkaakk'e Tribe • Huslia Village • Hydaburg Cooperative Association • Igiugig Village • Iipay
Slope • Ione Band of Miwok Indians • Iowa Tribe of Kansas and Nebraska • Iowa Tribe of Oklahoma • Iqurmuit Traditional Council • Isle
Choctaw Indians • Jicarilla Apache Nation • Juaneño Band of Mission Indians, Acjachemen Nation • Kaguyak Village • Kaibab Band of Paiute
Rancheria • Kaskigluk Traditional Elders Council • Kaw Nation • Kenaitze Indian Tribe • Ketchikan Indian Community • Kewa Pueblo • Keweenaw
• King Island Native Community • King Salmon Tribe • Kiowa Tribe • Klamath Tribes • Klawock Cooperative Association • Kletsel Dehe Band of
Village • Kootenai Tribe of Idaho • Koyukuk Native Village • La Jolla Band of Luiseño Indians • La Posta Band of Mission Indians • Lac Courte
Lake Superior Chippewa • Las Vegas Paiute Tribe • Lenape Indian Tribe of Delaware • Levelock Village • Lime Village • Lipan Apache Tribe •
• Lone Pine Paiute-Shoshone Tribe • Los Coyotes Band of Cahuilla and Cupeño Indians • Lovelock Paiute Tribe • Lower Brule Sioux Tribe •
• Ma-Chis Lower Creek Indian Tribe of Alabama • Mackinac Bands of Chippewa and Ottawa Indians • Makah Tribe • Manchester Band of
Manokotak Village • Manzanita Band of Kumeyaay Nation • Mashantucket (Western) Pequot Tribal Nation • Mashpee Wampanoag Tribe •
Mechoopda Indian Tribe of Chico Rancheria • Meherrin Nation • Menominee Indian Tribe of Wisconsin • Mentasta Traditional Council • Mesa
of Oklahoma • Miccosukee Tribe of Indians of Florida • Middletown Rancheria of Pomo Indians of California • Minnesota Chippewa Tribe
Choctaw Indians • Moapa Band of Paiutes • Modoc Tribe • Mohegan Tribe • Monacan Indian Nation • Mooretown Rancheria • Morongo Band of
Nation • Muscogee (Creek) • Muscogee Nation of Florida • Muwekma Ohlone Tribe of the San Francisco Bay Area • Naknek Native Village
Tribe of Louisiana • Native Tribe of Kanatak • Native Village of Afognak • Native Village of Akhiok • Native Village of Akutan • Native
Village of Bill Moore's Slough • Native Village of Brevig Mission • Native Village of Buckland • Native Village of Cantwell • Native Village
Native Village of Deering • Native Village of Diomede (Inalik) • Native Village of Eagle • Native Village of Eek • Native Village of Ekuk

Para Gladys,
mi mamá and
the keeper of
all recipes
—J.M.—N.

To Irs, Nana, and
all the women who
teach us stuff
—K.N.M.

# FRY BREAD

## A Native American Family Story

Written by
Kevin Noble Maillard

Roaring Brook Press
New York

Illustrated by
Juana Martinez-Neal

# FRY BREAD IS FOOD

Flour, salt, water
Cornmeal, baking powder
Perhaps milk, maybe sugar

All mixed together in a big bowl

# FRY BREAD IS SHAPE

Hands mold the dough

Flat like a pancake

Round like a ball

Or puffy like Nana's softest pillow

# FRY BREAD IS SOUND

The skillet clangs on the stove
The fire blazes from below
Drop the dough in the skillet
The bubbles sizzle and pop

# FRY BREAD IS COLOR

Golden brown, tan, or yellow

Deep like coffee, sienna, or earth

Light like snow and cream
Warm like rays of sun

# FRY BREAD IS FLAVOR

See beans or soup

Smell tacos, cheese, and vegetables

Delight in honey and jam

Rise to discover what brings us together

FRY BREAD IS TIME

On weekdays and holidays
Supper or dinner
Powwows and festivals
Moments together
With family and friends

# FRY BREAD IS ART

Sculpture, landscape, portrait
Our daily craft
Shared from teacher to student
A cycle of heritage and fortune

# FRY BREAD IS HISTORY

The long walk, the stolen land

Strangers in our own world

With unknown food

We made new recipes

From what we had

## FRY BREAD IS PLACE

Alaska, Kansas, all the way to Maine

Down to Delaware, on to Georgia

Over to Oklahoma, Colorado, and California

Cities and lands we call home

## FRY BREAD IS EVERYTHING

Round, flat, large, small

North, South, East, West

Brown, yellow, black, white

Familiar and foreign, old and new

We come together

# FRY BREAD IS US

We are still here
Elder and young
Friend and neighbor

We strengthen each other
To learn, change, and survive

FRY BREAD IS
YOU

# Kevin's Fry Bread

1 pint boiling water

1 cup cornmeal

1½ cups cold water

½ oz. of dry or instant yeast,
approx. 2 packages

1 cup raw sugar

1 tsp. sea salt

3½ cups flour

32 oz. unrefined coconut oil

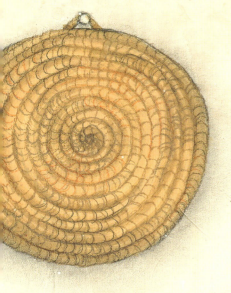

**1) Bring 1 pint of water** to a boil in a medium pot. Add cornmeal to boiling water. Whip slowly until smooth. Reduce heat to medium, add cold water, and cook until thick. Stir continuously to prevent lumps in the mixture. Remove from heat and let cool in pot.

**2) In a large bowl,** add yeast, sugar, and salt to the cooled cornmeal, along with small sprinkles of water to moisten the mixture. Gradually add flour, using a metal whisk or potato masher to get rid of lumps. Sprinkle water to keep dough moist but thick. Cover with a damp cloth and let rise for 3 hours.

**3) Once the dough has risen,** it should be springy and sticky. Heat the coconut oil in an iron skillet to medium temperature. Test the heat by dropping a small portion of dough into the oil. It should gently sizzle but not splatter. Use two large, oiled spoons to make golf ball–sized portions and dip immediately into the oil, submerging the entire ball. Re-oil the spoons in the skillet to make new balls of dough. Leave room in skillet, as the balls will expand in the hot oil.

**4) Let dough fry** until it cooks to your desired color: light golden or dark brown—about 3 minutes. Using tongs, flip balls over to cook the other side. Remove from oil and transfer to a paper towel–lined bowl, separating each level with a new paper towel. Eat while hot.

Father steadies the pan of hot oil as the children await the delicious food. They listen, smell, and hear the bread. To them, fry bread is like birthday cake or Halloween candy: a special treat to be cherished and savored.

Yet there are some Natives who strongly oppose fry bread because it exacerbates existing health problems. For these critics, fry bread is an easy target for a much larger problem of being forced to deviate from a traditional Indigenous diet.[4] Some, but not all, communities have no fresh market or a convenient place to buy fruits and vegetables.[5] Fast food is plentiful, cheap, and unhealthy. Access to quality health care and medical facilities may be difficult in underserved areas. Diabetes, obesity, and heart problems are longstanding problems.

Fry bread as a daily cuisine is no solution.[6] Like the previously mentioned birthday cake, fry bread is not an every-meal staple, like naan bread or jasmine rice. It is best enjoyed in moderation.

Even so, there aren't many healthy adaptations for fry bread, like baking instead of frying or replacing ingredients with low-calorie alternatives, so in keeping with those that came before me, I adjusted it. To fry the dough, I prefer unrefined coconut oil, which tastes better than the traditional lard or shortening. And it fills the kitchen with a wonderful aroma that announces the arrival of something special.

## FRY BREAD IS COLOR . . .

The population of Americans that identify as Native American is diverse and varied. Of the five million people identifying as American Indian or Alaska Native on the 2010 Census (out of a total of 308.7 million census respondents), slightly less than half, 2.2 million, claim that identity in combination with White or Black ancestry.[7] Today, over half of all people claiming Native ancestry marry and have children with people of a different race.

Most people think Native Americans always have brown skin and black hair. But there is an enormous range of hair textures and skin colors. Just like the characters in this book, Native people may have blonde hair or black skin, tight cornrows or a loose braid. This wide variety of faces reflects a history of intermingling between tribes and also with people of European, African, and Asian descent.

The racial aspect of being Native American differs from the political status of tribal membership, which is so different and so complicated across Indian country. Not all American Indians are enrolled as citizens of a tribal government. Some have never enrolled in any tribe, while some have been forcibly disenrolled. Additionally, each nation has different membership requirements based on blood and descent, which may be enough for one tribe,[8] but prevent similarly situated applicants from obtaining citizenship in another.[9] In addition, someone may be enrolled as a full-fledged member and never have any contact with Native culture.

So what makes a person American Indian? Blood? Enrollment? Physical appearance? Cultural ties? People that identify as Native American come in all colors and shapes and live in urban and rural areas. And many love to eat fry bread.

## FRY BREAD IS FLAVOR . . .

Everyone has a different opinion of what fry bread *should* be—everyone's a critic. Just like a strong opinion of the best barbecue or pizza, tastes are deeply personal, like one's own identity. The way I learned how to make fry bread in Wewoka, Oklahoma, was the *only way* to make fry bread. When I moved to Michigan in my mid-twenties, all those Midwestern Chippewas let me know how wrong I was—*theirs* was the only way, and it was also *the best*. It's literally a matter of taste.

Fry bread reflects the vast, deep diversity of Indian Country and there is no single way of making this special food. But it brings diverse Indigenous communities together through a shared culinary and cultural experience. That's the beauty of fry bread.

The ceramic pot on the left page copies the geometric pattern commonly found on ceremonial sashes worn by Seminoles around their waists or over their shoulders. These colorful zigzags may also be found on patchwork skirts, shawls, and jackets. Blues, reds, oranges, purples, greens, and yellows make beautiful rainbows and patterns in these tribal fabrics and crafts.

## FRY BREAD IS TIME . . .

Most Native families have a "fry bread lady," usually a grandmother or an old aunt who holds a special recipe that she passes on to her female successor.

In my family, two aunts competed for the title. My Aunt (we say "ahwnt") Fannie was the "town" aunt and a fan of complicated recipes, so her version of fry bread was culinary, scientific, and definitely better. Maggie, her sister, was the "country" aunt and runner-up to the bread battle, but lived to ninety-nine, long after her gourmand sister.

But once Aunt Maggie started to burn the fry, I took over. No one else was taking it up, and I wanted to learn. Family dinners and holidays were always fun, but definitely less tasty without fry bread. The first few batches were long, messy learning moments, but now, my family and friends request it at every opportunity.

Gender requirements aside, I became that "lady."

## FRY BREAD IS ART . . .

The handmade dolls and coil baskets featured on this spread are part of a rich inherited history of both the Seminole Nation of Oklahoma and the Seminole Tribe of Florida. After the Great Depression, tribal members in Florida opened tourist villages and sold handicrafts as an alternate source of income during a period of economic insecurity. Enterprising Seminoles sold crafts, fabrics, and keepsakes to visitors to the villages. Dolls dressed in traditional clothing were a signature souvenir.

Dollmaking grew into a cultural tradition passed from ancestors to their descendants, like a grandmother teaching a grandchild. The doll bodies held by the children on the right page can be made from the fronds of a palmetto tree or sweetgrass leaves. The dolls may also have elaborate beadwork sewn together from tiny glass balls to form different patterns. Traditional Seminole patchwork designs are shown on the dolls' clothing and also on the sitting woman's skirt, with bright stripes of all colors.

The large baskets shown on the left page have many purposes: holding fruit, cleaning vegetables, hauling wood, protecting valuables, or anything else that could fit inside. Baskets may also be purely interesting to admire and share with others. Before the creators begin, they make sure they have plenty of leaves or fronds to weave into tight coils. The baskets may be colorfully decorated, either with paint or by weaving different leaf shades into the pattern.

The craft of basket weaving is also shared by coastal African American communities in the South, with whom the Seminoles have a long and intertwined history.

## FRY BREAD IS HISTORY . . .

Native Americans are Indigenous peoples, meaning they are descendants of the original inhabitants of the country we know as the United States.[10] When Europeans made first contact, there were violent, bloody struggles for control of the land. Colonists stole property and killed people who had lived here for thousands of years. In contrast to the amicable relations taught at school and celebrated at home every Thanksgiving, the vast majority of relations between Indian nations and the American government have been marked by war, genocide, and conflict. Antagonism, while not as violent, persists to the present day.

Under President Andrew Jackson, the government evicted Southeastern tribes from their homelands under the Indian Removal Act of 1830. American soldiers forced entire families out of their ancestral lands, took all of their belongings, and made them walk across the country to lands unseen in the West.

This fateful resettlement, where thousands of people died along the way, was endured by many Indian nations, and in some it is known as the "Trail of Tears."

Removal and displacement of Native Americans occurred—and is still occurring—in every state in the country. Pequots lost land to colonists in 1638 Connecticut. The Sac & Fox fought with Europeans for their land in the Great Lakes region and now have reserves in Oklahoma, Kansas, and Nebraska.[11] Mid-century Indian termination and relocation policies sought to dissolve tribal nations with a goal of destroying sovereignty and assimilating members into mainstream society. This resulted in the termination of over one hundred tribes and the loss of over 1.3 million acres of land.[12] And in 2017, the Standing Rock Sioux protested the federal government's support of construction of the Dakota Access Pipeline on tribal land in North Dakota and surrounding states.[13]

## FRY BREAD IS PLACE . . .

The map shown on this spread goes beyond the borders of the United States. The lines you're used to seeing drawn between states and countries have been left out since they are federal demarcations that came after the creation and preexistence of tribal lands.

Some Native Americans live on tribal land and others live in cities. The majority live outside of reserved areas, about 78 percent according to the 2010 Census. The largest reservation, the Navajo, was home to almost 174,000 people, and in New York City alone, there were over 111,000 Native people.[14]

## FRY BREAD IS NATION . . .

At the time of this book's publication, there are 573 federally recognized Native American tribes in the United States. There are also 67 state-recognized tribes. (In Canada there are over 600!) Recognition means that the United States government or a state government has acknowledged the tribe as a sovereign entity, much like France establishing diplomatic relations with Nigeria.

The recognition process is very long, and each tribe is required to prove that they have a shared history, a shared culture, a strong government, and a common origin, among other things. This can be very difficult since so many tribes have suffered from immense amounts of relocation and cultural stripping. Sometimes, a group applies for federal and state recognition, but is denied by both, even though they are Native Americans whose ancestors have been in North America for thousands of years. When the personal opinion of being Native differs from the political opinion of being Native, it brings up hard questions about who and what counts as authentically Indian.[15]

In the spirit of inclusivity and as a celebration of Native pride, the list in this book gives voice to the Indigenous nations and communities within the United States. This includes large tribes like the Navajo and the Choctaw, smaller tribes like the Kickapoo and the Duckwater Shoshone, rancherias in California like Shingle Springs and Pinoleville, and Alaskan Native villages like Kwigillingok and Mary's Igloo. This list also includes groups who were not successful in their attempts to achieve official status with the U.S. or state governments, like the Duwamish or the Little Shell Chippewa. In the pages and end pages of this book, however, they are recognized.

We researched or reached out to each nation listed here to confirm the common usage of their tribal name. We wanted to be as accurate as possible and to include tribes in the process.

## FRY BREAD IS EVERYTHING . . .

Bread nourishes and comforts in so many cultures, religions, and communities around the world. Its synonyms speak of sustenance and survival: dough, manna, money, life. They are loaves and

leavens, bagels and braids, crepes and cakes. They are communions, meant to be shared and loved with others, because bread is not meant to be cooked for one.

## FRY BREAD IS US . . .

While so much of United States federal policy has acted to weaken Indigenous governments and undermine tribal sovereignty, Native nations continue to exist and demand recognition of their endurance and strength by the United States. Native America is not a past history of vanished people and communities. *We are still here.*

## WE STRENGTHEN EACH OTHER . . .

If you look closely at the kitchen cabinet, you can see names and doodles etched into the side. Each of the names included are people that have been involved in the creation of the book, along with some family members. Juana's children, Ethan, Aidan, and Eva, hand wrote the names.

The picture hanging in the kitchen and also on the right of the recipe page is my Aunt Fannie, who taught me how to make fry bread her way, without reservation.

## Reference

Vine Deloria, Jr., *Custer Died for Your Sins: An Indian Manifesto* (University of Oklahoma Press, 1969)

Dorothy Downs, *Art of the Florida Seminole and Miccosukee Indians* (University Press of Florida, 1995)

William Lorenz Katz, *Black Indians: A Hidden Heritage* (Atheneum Books for Young Readers, 2012)

## Notes

[1] newsmaven.io/indiancountrytoday/archive
frybread-101-a-basic-recipe-and-timeline-bhnPNWvNAEutnZGldYjKYw

[2] seminolenationmuseum.org

[3] These patterns are usually found in fabric and jewelry, like skirts, blankets, or necklaces.

[4] Devon Mihesuah, "Indigenous Health Initiatives, Frybread, and the Marketing of Nontraditional 'Traditional' American Indian Foods." *Native American and Indigenous Studies* 3. no. 45. (2016): 45-69

[5] A food desert is defined by the American Nutrition Association as, "parts of the country vapid of fresh fruit, vegetables, and other healthful whole foods, usually found in impoverished areas." socialwork.tulane.edu/blog/food-deserts-in-america

[6] Suzan Shown Harjo, "My New Year's Resolution: No More Fat 'Indian' Food," Indian Country Today, January 26, 2005. newsmaven.io/indiancountrytoday/archive
my-new-year-s-resolution-no-more-fat-indian-food-M6Fd3dv8tkWPjg383hjFyA

[7] U.S. Census, The American Indian and Alaska Native Population: 2010. census.gov/history/pdf/c2010br-10.pdf

[8] Kevin Noble Maillard, "Elizabeth Warren's Birther Moment," *New York Times*, May 4, 2012. campaignstops.blogs.nytimes.com/2012/05/04/elizabeth-warrens-birther-moment

[9] William Glaberson, "Who is a Seminole, and Who Gets to Decide?" *New York Times*, January 29, 2001. nytimes.com/2001/01/29/us/who-is-a-seminole-and-who-gets-to-decide.html

[10] Charles C. Mann, 1491: *New Revelations of the Americas Before Columbus* (Knopf, 2005).

[11] Sac & Fox history, sacandfoxks.com/history/tribe

[12] iltf.org/land-issues/issues

[13] James Estrin, "Land, Loss and Rebirth in Standing Rock," *New York Times*, September 4, 2017. lens.blogs.nytimes.com/2017/09/04/land-loss-and-rebirth-in-standing-rock

[14] U.S. Census, The American Indian and Alaska Native Population: 2010. census.gov/history/pdf/c2010br-10.pdf

[15] Broke Jarvis, "Who Decides Who Counts as Native American?" *New York Times*, January 18, 2017.

Native Village of Ekwok · Native Village of Elim · Native Village of Eyak (Cordova) · Native Village of False Pass · Native Village of · Native Village of Hooper Bay · Native Village of Karluk · Native Village of Kiana · Native Village of Kipnuk · Native Village of Kotzebue · Native Village of Koyuk · Native Village of Kwigillingok · Native Village of Kwinhagak · Native Village of Larsen Bay · Native Village of Nanwalek (English Bay) · Native Village of Napaimute · Native Village of Napakiak · Native Village of Napaskiak · of Nuiqsut · Native Village of Nunam Iqua · Native Village of Nunapitchuk · Native Village of Ouzinkie · Native Village of Paimiut · Village of Point Lay · Native Village of Port Graham · Native Village of Port Heiden · Native Village of Port Lions · Native Village · Native Village of Shaktoolik · Native Village of Shishmaref · Native Village of Shungnak · Native Village of South Naknek · Native · Native Village of Teller · Native Village of Tetlin · Native Village of Tuntutuliak · Native Village of Tununak · Native Village of Tyonek · Mountain · Navajo (Diné) Nation · Nenana Native Association · New Koliganek Village Council · New Stuyahok Village · Newtok Village · Community · Nondalton Village · Nooksack Indian Tribe · Noorvick Native Community · North Fork Rancheria of Mono Indians · Huron Band of the Potawatomi · Nottoway Indian Tribe of Virginia · Nulato Village · Nulhegan Band of the Coosuk Abenaki Nation · Oneida Indian Nation · Oneida Nation · Onondaga Nation · Organized Village of Grayling (Holikachuk) · Organized Village of Kake · Osage Nation · Oscarville Traditional Village · Otoe-Missouria Tribe · Ottawa Tribe of Oklahoma · Paiute Indian Tribe of Utah · Tribe—Indian Township Reservation · Passamaquoddy Tribe—Pleasant Point Reservation · Patawomeck Indian Tribe of Virginia · Indians · Pedro Bay Village · Pee Dee Indian Tribe of South Carolina · Pee Dee Nation of Upper South Carolina · Penobscot Nation · Lower Eastern Cherokee Nation South Carolina · Pilot Station Traditional Village · Pinoleville Pomo Nation · Piqua Shawnee Tribe · Piscataway · of the Pokanoket Nation · Pointe-au-Chien Indian Tribe · Pokagon Band of Potawatomi · Ponca Tribe of Nebraska · Ponca Tribe of · Potawatomi Nation · Prairie Island Indian Community · Praying Indians of Natick · Pueblo de San Ildefonso · Pueblo of Acoma · Pueblo of · of Santa Ana · Pueblo of Zia · Pueblo of Zuni · Puyallup Tribe of Indians · Pyramid Lake Paiute Tribe · Qagan Tayagungin Tribe of · Indian Nation · Ramapough Lunaape Nation · Ramona Band of Cahuilla · Rampart Village · Rappahannock Tribe · Red Cliff Band of · Valley · Reno-Sparks Indian Colony · Resighini Rancheria · Rincon Band of Luiseño Indians · Robinson Rancheria of Pomo Indians · Oklahoma · Sac & Fox Tribe of the Mississippi in Iowa · Saginaw Chippewa Indian Tribe · Saint Regis Mohawk Tribe · Salt River · Band of Mission Indians · San Pasqual Band of Mission Indians · Santa Clara Pueblo · Santa Rosa Band of Cahuilla Indians · Santa · Carolina · Santee Sioux Nation · Sappony · Sauk-Suiattle Indian Tribe · Sault Ste. Marie Tribe of Chippewa Indians · Schaghticoke · Oklahoma · Seminole Tribe of Florida · Seneca Nation of Indians · Seneca-Cayuga Nation · Shageluk Native Village · Shakopee · Shingle Springs Band of Miwok Indians · Shinnecock Indian Nation · Shoalwater Bay Tribe · Shoshone-Bannock Tribes · Shoshone- · of Alaska · Skagway Village · Skokomish Indian Tribe · Skull Valley Band of Goshute · Snoqualmie Indian Tribe · Soboba Band of · Spirit Lake Tribe · Spokane Tribe of Indians · Squaxin Island Tribe · St. Croix Chippewa Indians of Wisconsin · Standing Rock · Mohican Indians · Summit Lake Paiute Tribe · Sumter Tribe of Cheraw Indians · Sun'aq Tribe of Kodiak · Suquamish Tribe · Susanville · Band of the Kumeyaay Nation · Table Mountain Rancheria · Tachi-Yokut Tribe · Takotna Village · Tangirnaq Native Village · Taos · Thlopthlocco Tribal Town · Timbisha Shoshone Tribe · Tohono O'odham Nation · Tolowa Dee-ni' Nation · Tonawanda Band of Seneca · River Indian Tribe · Tuluksak Native Community · Tunica-Biloxi Tribe of Louisiana · Tuolumne Band of Me-Wuk Indians · Turtle · Traditional Village · Umkumiut Native Village · United Auburn Indian Community · United Cherokee AniYunWiYa Nation · United Houma Nation · Skagit Tribe · Ute Indian Tribe · Ute Mountain Ute Tribe · Utu Utu Gwaitu Paiute Tribe · Viejas Band of Kumeyaay Indians · Village of · Crooked Creek · Village of Dot Lake · Village of Iliamna · Village of Kalskag · Village of Kaltag · Village of Kotlik · Village of Lower Kalskag · Village of Sun'aq Tribe of Kodiak · Village of Venetie · Village of Wainwright · Waccamaw Indian People · Waccamaw Siouan Tribe · Walker · Webster / Dudley Band of the Chaubunagungamaug Nipmuck · White Mountain Apache Tribe · Wichita and Affiliated Tribes · Wilton · Yakutat Tlingit Tribe · Yankton Sioux Tribe · Yavapai-Apache Nation · Yavapai-Prescott Indian Tribe · Yerington Paiute Tribe · Yocha Dehe